Prologue

This story begins in late 1947, at a dinner hosted by Nicholas and his wife, Zoe. They invited all the world leaders who had helped with cease-fires and in other ways to make it possible for Christmas gifts to be delivered during World War II and smaller conflicts that lingered afterwards. One of the guests, Gen. DeGaulle told Nicholas he wanted to invite him and Zoe to Paris, as guests of France, to enjoy the beautiful city as appreciation for the work done by Nicholas and his team every Christmas.

Some years went by, and in 1959 the time seemed right for the visit.

Raspinel	ras PIN' el
Zoe	ZO' ee
Yvonne	ee VON'
Elysee	el EE' zay
Moulan Rouge	moo lan ROOZH'
Le Marias	lay MA ray

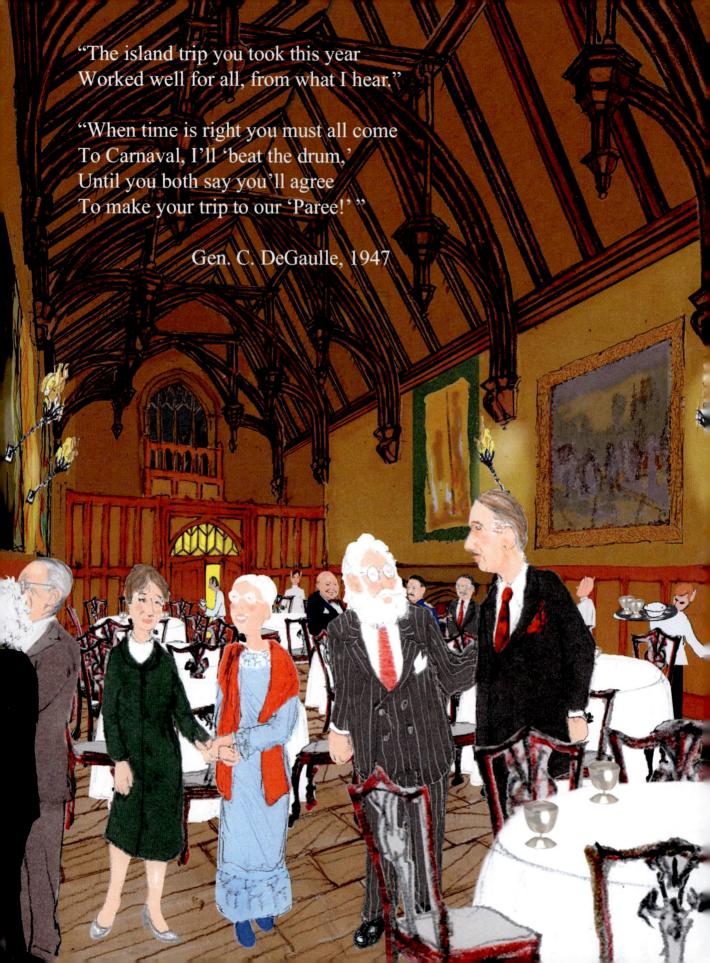

"The island trip you took this year
Worked well for all, from what I hear."

"When time is right you must all come
To Carnaval, I'll 'beat the drum,'
Until you both say you'll agree
To make your trip to our 'Paree!'"

Gen. C. DeGaulle, 1947

"Nick, a letter from Charles DeGalle,
An invitation for us all!
He brought this up some time ago,
He said he'd ask us, and it's so."

"Aya, your French, it's very good!
Your note has made this understood!
We'll go to Paris! DeGaulle's guests!
That means you, too - your French is best!"

Paris, 12 Janvier 1959

Cher Nicolas,

Je tiens à vous et votre charmante épouse inviter à Paris pour le Carnaval en Mars.

Si vous ne pouvez assister à au moins quelques jours, nous aurions beaucoup profiter de votre entreprise et l'occasion de vous remercier pour tout ce que vous faites.

S'il vous plaît aviser le numéro dans votre entourage. Le plus on est de fous!

C. de Gaulle

Son Excellence
Monsieur Nicholas de Myra
Nikolai Fjord, Norway

Dear Nicholas, I wish to invite you and your lovely wife to Paris for the Carnival this March.

If you can attend for at least a few days, we would much enjoy your company and the opportunity to thank you for all you do.

Please advise the number in your entourage. The more the merrier!

C. de Gaulle

So very nice, to take things slow,
And see so much, when flying low!
Weather's perfect - in two more days
We'll enjoy Paris' lovely ways!

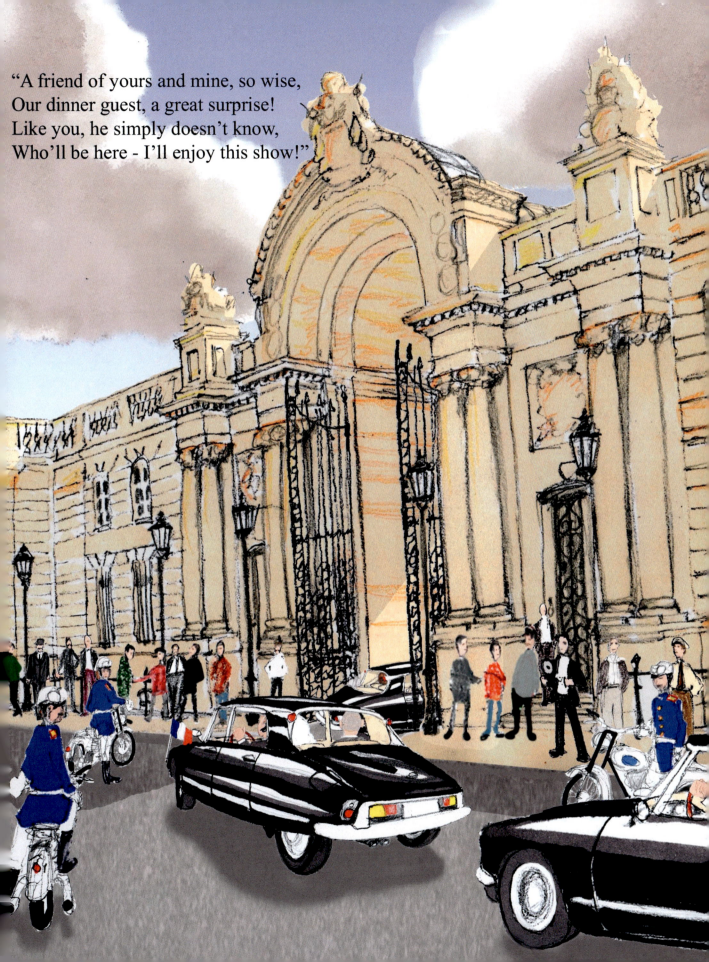

"A friend of yours and mine, so wise,
Our dinner guest, a great surprise!
Like you, he simply doesn't know,
Who'll be here - I'll enjoy this show!"

Soon, it was the dinner hour.
The surprise - the Eisenhowers!

The presidents joked, as presidents can,
About many things, but not either man,
Failed to remember their awe of St. Nick
When he'd come ask them to make ceasefires stick!

"Oh, the history this place marks,
Nick, it's said you've flown through the Arc?"
"Charles, that sounds so childish, I fear,
But, yes, it happens once a year."

After church, this seventh day,
A fine stroll through Le Marias.
Downhill toward the river Seine,
A morning no one could complain.

Poodles, Bulldogs, and Bichons, too,
The dogs all want their ribbons Blue!
This dog show is a great event -
The grooming surely costs a mint!

DeGaulle had business at noon,
A picnic lunch seemed opportune.
Within the lovely springtime air
The day was perfect everywhere.

Mechanics with the airship crew
Paid little mind to what cats do.
The rascals climbed up to the deck,
They'd seen provisions they should check.

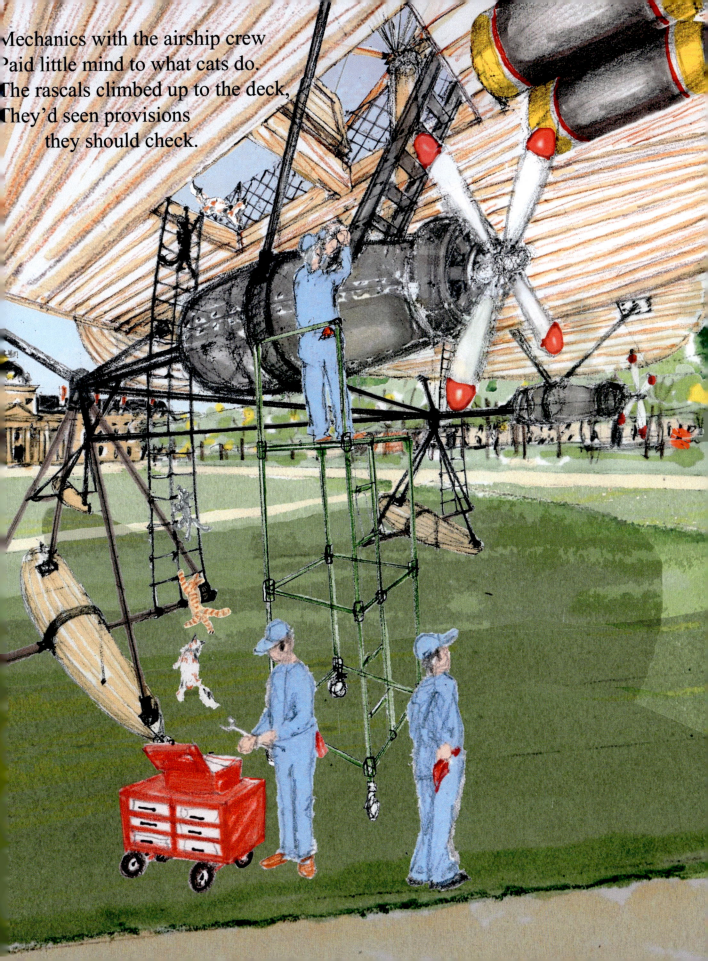

Sure enough, with practiced ease,
They found new boxes of Brie cheese!

Oooh! Stowie saw a shiny thing,
He landed on it with a spring.
He lost his balance when he lit,
And felt a lever give a bit...

A funny sound came to his ear.
He felt a sudden twinge of fear.
The airship heaved and snapped its stays.
It slowly rose a little ways.

The airship's loose! A great alarm!
Do something - fast - so no one's harmed!
Nick knew the owls were the one chance
To save this lovely trip to France

The thought came to Raspinel, too.
The owls were told what they must do.
They had to catch the airship, quick,
And lift the lever, no small trick!

Now both the little owls gave chase,
Their flight was rapid, full of grace.
They had to bring the airship down,
But not 'til it was out of town.

Once outside town, to Neon's mind,
As good as any place they'd find,
He grasped the lever in his claws
And pulled and pulled and didn't pause.

They drifted down in countryside.
The cats decided they should hide.
Now close to ground, the pair of owls
Could see they'd land in a canal.

Gendarmes arrived with much ado,
And Stowie noticed St. Nick, too.
Afraid now for his furry skin,
He glanced toward St. Nick again.

Stowie said, "Maui, what to do?"
The Paris cats bid them adieu.

It's great to see the cats are OK,
But a dinner's planned at Elysee.
Nick knew that they would be in trouble
If they weren't back - and on the double!

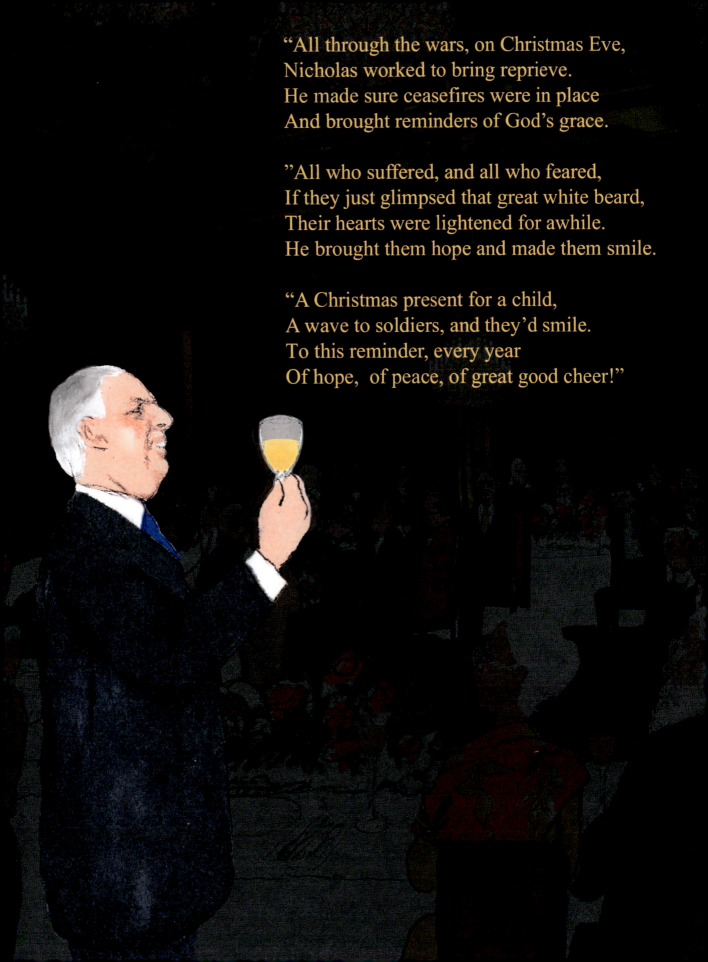

"All through the wars, on Christmas Eve,
Nicholas worked to bring reprieve.
He made sure ceasefires were in place
And brought reminders of God's grace.

"All who suffered, and all who feared,
If they just glimpsed that great white beard,
Their hearts were lightened for awhile.
He brought them hope and made them smile.

"A Christmas present for a child,
A wave to soldiers, and they'd smile.
To this reminder, every year
Of hope, of peace, of great good cheer!"

MAP OF TRIP

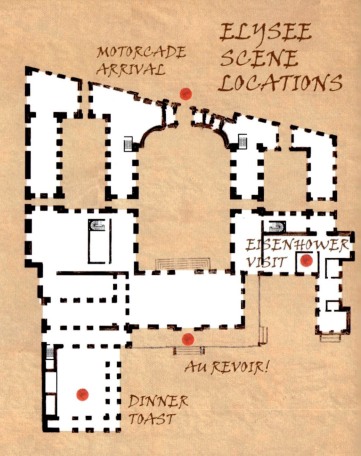

ELYSEE SCENE LOCATIONS

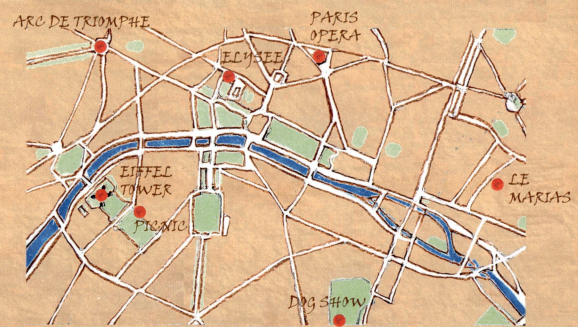

THE BOOK'S SCENE LOCATIONS IN PARIS

A New Airship
September, 1920
Nicholai Fjord, Norway

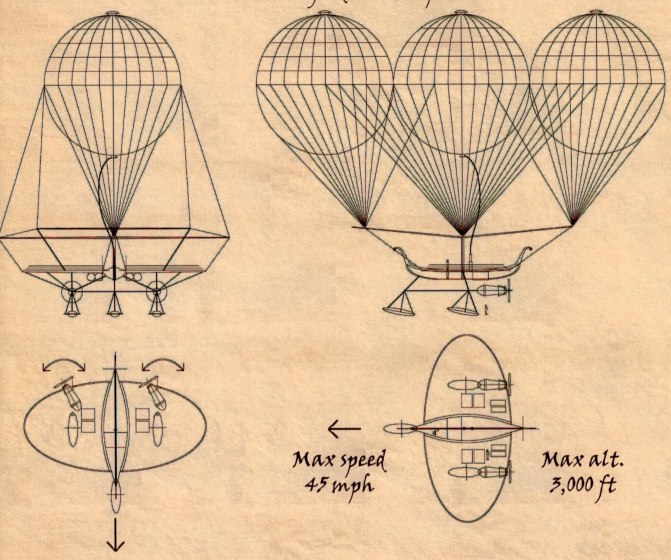

Max speed 45 mph

Max alt. 3,000 ft

Helium is pumped into balloons for lift.
Air is pumped into balloons to lower the ship.
Levers are housed beside the ship's wheel
to control the amount of air or helium,
hence the ship's altitude.
Forward motion is produced by motors, which
turn propellers. The motor assemblies turn
left to right to steer the ship.
The ship may take off or land on water or on land.

Also by Russell Claxton

THE ST. NICHOLAS YORKIES
SAVING CHRISTMAS DAY

A Christmas tale of near-disaster, and a spirited response from the people and dogs of York.

The story will probably delight anyone who's ever known a dog.

Or a reindeer.

Or a cat.

ST. NICHOLAS AND FRIENDS
THE WHOLE YEAR ROUND

Come along for the ride! See how St. Nicholas and friends spend the year of 1947 having fun and getting ready for the long night's work on Christmas Eve.

THE ST. NICHOLAS OWLS
AND THE LUCKIEST LAB

From a pair of unearthly eggs to a sharp-eyed rescue, the owls bring a new dimension to the St. Nicholas team in Tromso, and a new Labrador puppy.

ST. NICHOLAS AND THE DOGS OF ROME

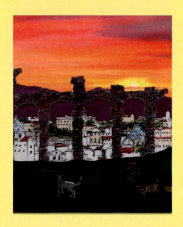

1954. Eight years after recruiting 44 Yo to save Christmas Day, Sally is going t college with a scholarship in Rome. Al with her studies, she continues a new-found interest in rescuing dogs.

www.blueigloobooks.com

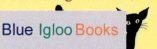

About the author

Russell Claxton, a Texas native, has called Macon, Georgia home for over twenty-five years with his wife Natalie and a string of dogs, cats and wildlife.

He is a practicing architect and urban designer. The conservation of natural resources runs high on his list of priorities.

Animal well-being is a life-long preoccupation, with accompanying enjoyment and appreciation of dogs, cats and lots of other animal friends.

Made in United States
Orlando, FL
13 November 2023

38915559R00027